Not nice

Open oyster

Paint
the pail

Quilt a quilt

Rubber raft

Smelly shoe

Trollusk tears

Unusually
unlucky

Very vain
vampire

Wash
the walrus

Xray

Your yellow yarn

Zipperump-a-zoo

Little Monster®

Word Book with Mother Goose

By Mercer Mayer

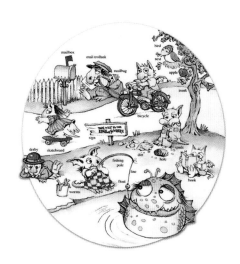

Published by FastPencil PREMIERE
307 Orchard City Drive, Suite 210, Campbell CA 95008
Premiere.FastPencil.com

Mercer Mayer's
Little Monster®

mailbox

mail trollusk

mailbag

bird

nest

apple

trunk

bicycle

THIS WAY TO THE EDGE OF NOWHERE

sign

skateboard

derby

spade

dirt

hole

book

fishing pole

line

float

worms

Word Book

Letters

Angry

anchovy

Big bite

Cup of cola

Down the drain

Eat everything

Fetch the fiddle

Give a grin

Hold him

It is icky

Jumping
jack-in-the-box

Kicking
kerploppus

Leaping
lizards

Much
mud

Not nice

Open oyster

Paint the pail

Quilt a quilt

Rubber raft

Smelly shoe

Trollusk tears

Unusually unlucky

Very vain vampire

Wash the walrus

Xray

Your yellow yarn

Zipperump-a-zoo

5

cymbals

WASHTUB BAND

saw

comb and
tissue paper

tuba

EDGE OF NOWHERE MARCHING BAND

ukulele

trombone

saxophone

clarinet

tambourine

trumpet

microphone

**MARCHING
BAND**

electric guitar

maracas

cymbal

snare drum   bass fiddle

speaker

ROCK AND ROLL BAND

6

washboard

washtub bass

bow

fiddle

kazoo

guitar

harmonica

five-string banjo

COWBOY CRITTER and his WACKY WACKY BAND

flute

drumsticks

batons

parade snare drum

baton twirlers

drum major

Music

7

roller coaster

County Fair

barn

silo

prize tomato

farmer

tractor

rooster

BUMPER CARS

cow

goat

sheep

horse

RIDE THE DONKEY AND GET YOUR PICTURE TAKEN

SHOOTING GALLERY

HIT THE BOTTLE

Teddy bears

pinwheel

milk bottles

cotton candy

camera

photographer

win-a-prize booths

8

Ferris wheel

TEST YOUR MUSCLES

bell

pinwheel

HOME MADE

cake   bread   pie

jams and jellies

mallet

RIDE A KERPLOPPUS MERRY-GO-ROUND

Catch a Greased Kerploppus

cotton candy seller

cone

ice cream

scale

50 60 70 80 90 100 40 30 20 10

I WILL GUESS YOUR WEIGHT OR YOU WIN A BEAN BAG

foot-long hot dog

TICKETS

weight-guessing trollusk

ticket booth

9

thunder lizard
(brontosaurus)

little
kitty cat

big kitty cat

This big bird is
called a pterodactyl.
I bet you a piece
of bubble gum you
can't say that.

That!

parrot

fish

goldfish

flea

cricket

hamster

white mice

10

The Great Pet Show

pet bat

pet flower

lizard

turtle

zipperump-a-zoo

pet snake

worm

puppy fydolagump

first-prize ribbon

puppy dog

pet shoe

pet-judging trollusk

(If you were the judge, who would get first prize?)

bone

Games

catcher's mask

catcher

bat

baseball?

ball

batter

mitt

BASEBALL

pitcher

JACKS

jacks

CHECKERS

bird

winner

loser

checkers

checkerboard

birdie

racket

net

BADMINTON

hoop

net

basketball

croquet ball

wicket

mallet

CROQUET

BASKETBALL

hider

12

pins

bowling ball

BOWLING

bowler

football

catch

CARDS

Who is right?

GUESSING

seeker

"it"

TAG

target

shooter

ring

helmet

kick

dart

MARBLES

HIDE AND SEEK

DARTS

FOOTBALL

13

Things to Do With Paper

FOLD IT

paper airplane

hat

CUT IT

paper doll chain

scraps (throw them away)

scissors

WAD IT UP

newspaper

DRAW A PICTURE

crayon

pencil

ballpoint pen

MAKE A MASK

MAKE A PAPER CHAIN

WRITE A LETTER

Dear Billy, can you read yet.

paper with lines

clothespins

rope

string to tie it on

crayon

scissors (always be careful with scissors)

construction paper or cardboard

flashlight

paste

PASTE A PICTURE

sheet

MAKE A SHADOW-PUPPET SHOW

MAKE A FLOWER

heavy paper or cardboard

stick

tape

shadow puppet

Birthday Party

balloons

paper lanterns

egg-and-spoon race

punch bowl

ladle

egg

camera

sack race

party hat

noise-makers

birthday boy

Pin the Tail on the Kerploppus

birthday cake

paper cup

party favor

bowl

plate

fork

shirt

tablecloth

presents

jigsaw puzzle

ice cream and cake

15

Spooky Times

bat

looking for something in the attic

What is your favorite spooky time?

moon

clouds

hearing the wind howl

owl

passing an empty house

watching a scary TV show

looking for something in the cellar

taking out the garbage

furnace

mouse

Weather

raindrops

umbrella

RAIN

hailstones

HAIL

snowflakes

icicles

SNOW

SUNNY

lightning

THUNDERSTORM

FOG

TORNADO

WINDY

hot dog

hot-dog-
snatching bombanat

tree house

bird

butterfly

lean-to

outdoor
fireplace

flashlight

camper

CAMPING

backpack

canteen

sleeping b

hatchett

anthill

ants

tent

cattails

radio

picnic basket

rowboat

oar

Thermos
bottle

frog

lily pad

cold milk

bench

picnic table

PICNIC

18

Summertime

kite

turning somersaults

kite string

HAY RIDE

fishing pole

can of worms

bathing cap

swimming trunks

swimming suit

FISHING

WATER SKIING

water skis

diving board

sail

mast

SWIMMING

pond

BOATING

sailboat

T-shirt flag

snow castle

ski lift

SLEDDING

snow shovel

snow

gloves

jacket

snowballs

SNOWBALL FIGHT

sled

top hat

sticks

ice fangs

Thermos bottle

hot chocolate

figure skates

BUILDING A SNOW MONSTER

ICE SKATING

20

Wintertime

SKIING

skis

ski poles

ski boots

SLEIGH RIDE

icicles

ICE HOCKEY

hockey stick

ICE FISHING

snowsuit

puck

mittens

bench

hole

line

fish

mast

frozen pond

sail

boots

ICE BOATING

earmuffs

stocking cap

scarf

runner

Holidays

witch

false nose

candy bags

devil

skeleton

jack o'lantern

VALENTINE'S DAY

hearts

Make your own valentine!

red paper

paste

paper lace

scissors

EASTER

Easter-bunny suit

coloring eggs

yellow

green

red

eggs

purple

chocolate bunny

jelly beans

Easter basket

THANKSGIVING

roast turkey

pumpkin pie

blunderbuss

Pilgrim

Pilgrim

turkey

22

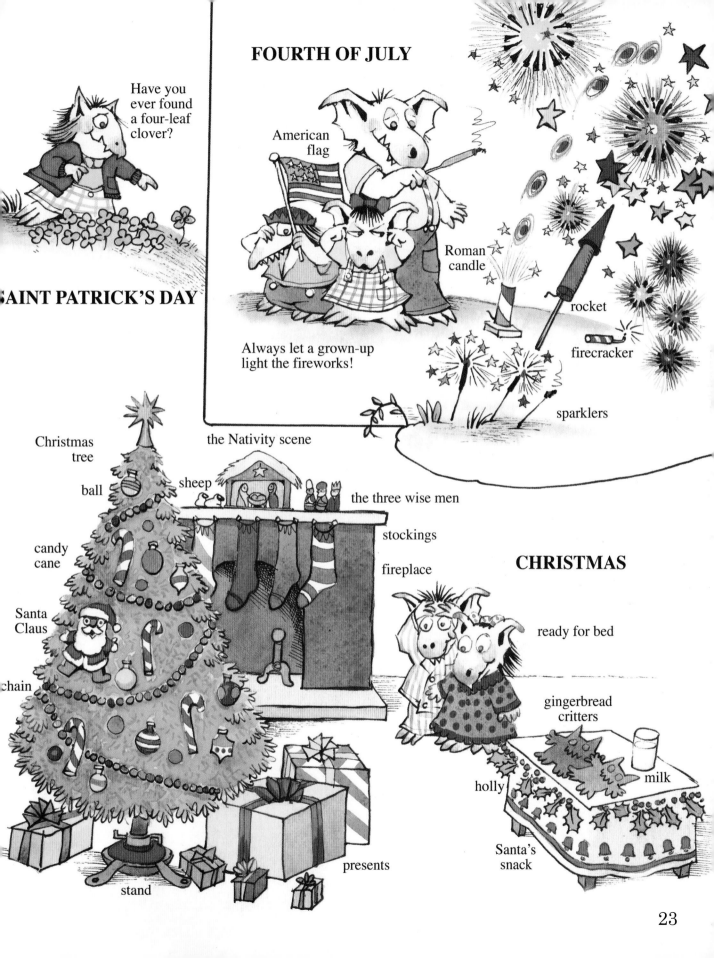

Have you ever found a four-leaf clover?

SAINT PATRICK'S DAY

FOURTH OF JULY

American flag

Roman candle

rocket

firecracker

Always let a grown-up light the fireworks!

sparklers

the Nativity scene

Christmas tree

ball

sheep

the three wise men

stockings

CHRISTMAS

candy cane

fireplace

Santa Claus

ready for bed

chain

gingerbread critters

holly

milk

Santa's snack

presents

stand

23

Ways to Travel

FREE BURGERS TODAY ONLY AT PETE'S PLACE

YOU'LL LIKE THEM

GET 'UM WHILE THEY LAST

WELCOME

use your wings

helicopter

sailboat

paper cup

Pete

motorcycle

raft

unicycle

Island Joe's RENT-A-TRAILER

END OF THE LINE

red wagon

car

house trailer

bus

tricycle

baby buggy

bicycle

hand print

by hands

24

balloon

UFO

jet

tugboat

rowboat

oar

rubber horse

swim

submarine

canoe

by elephant

paddle

by wheels

diesel train

EDGE OF NOWHERE OR BUST

on horseback

covered wagon

by feet

footprints

25

Moving Day

MONSTER MOVERS

GOLDEN

ask about our low rates

moving van

VAN
WE ARE GOOD

BOY, OH BOY, OH BOY, WOW!

WE WILL MOVE YOU OR A ZOO ANYWHERE ANY TIME ANY PLACE EVEN TO THE EDGE OF NOWHERE

SEAL OF GOODNESS

new friends

sofa

picture

rabbit ears

hand truck

ramp

grandfather clock

vacuum cleaner

la sh

moving carton

Have you ever rolled downhill in an empty moving carton?

antique table

lamp

boxes of books

potted palm

chimney

roof

old picture
frames

old radio

dress form

steamer trunk

ATTIC

BEDROOM

BEDROOM

mover

iron

light
switch

radiator

rug

LIVING
ROOM

pillow
mattress

mirror

wastebasket

mantel

fireplace

bed

box
of toys

dresser

record
player

easy chair

hassock

DINING ROOM

hanging the
drapes

pans

KITCHEN

unpacking
the dishes

refrigerator

dining
table

spade

chair

stove

ironing
board

rocking
chair

skateboard

27

Secret Hiding Places

INSIDE

in the closet

under the covers

under the bed

behind the sofa

in the dark

in the sofa

behind the curtains

behind a chair

under a newspaper

under a lamp shade

28

OUTSIDE

in a bush

behind a tree

behind a rock

in a blanket tent

in a hollow tree trunk

in a hole
in the ground

in a cardboard
carton clubhouse

under the
porch steps

NOT in the
garbage can

29

lawn mower

rake

nozzle

hose

MOWING THE GRASS

RAKING LEAVES

WATERING THE FLOWERS

sponge

hedge clippers

WASHING THE CAR

pail

TRIMMING THE HEDGE

dishes

Helping

HANGING UP YOUR CLOTHES

coat hangars

SETTING THE TABLE

closet

PUTTING AWAY YOUR BOOKS

head of the bed

bookcase

TYING LITTLE BROTHER'S SHOES

MAKING THE BED

broom

CLEANING UP OUR ROOM

toy chest

foot of the bed

Feelings

happy   jealous   sad

selfish

sharing

greedy

mad

31

First Times

first letter

first fish

first A

first bull's-eye

first electric
train set

32

first telephone call

first home run

first camp out

first tooth
to come out

first bicycle

first puppy

Things to Do or Be When You Get Bigger

farmer

truck driver

firefighter

police officer

doctor

gas station attendant

baker

storekeeper

astronaut

mail carrier

photographer

artist

skin diver

author

telephone operator

librarian

dentist

cabinetmaker

optician

florist

bird watcher

general

veterinarian

sailor

animal trainer

waiter

magician

juggler

taxi driver

actor

actress

hobo

Lessons

sheet music

PIANO

tutu

toe shoes

BALLET

tap shoes

TAP

KARATE

swimming trunks

SWIMMING

hunting cap

saddle

bridle

RIDING

mask

fencing swords

chest protector

FENCING

TENNIS

tennis ball

tennis racket

net

intbrush

canvas

model

easel

palette

PAINTING

POTTERY

potter's wheel

CLAY

sculpting tools

beret

smock

VIOLIN

BAGPIPE

COOKING

pan

spoon

apron

mixing bowl

GROWL

SNEER

BOO

SCARING LESSONS

Colors

RED

mix: **RED + YELLOW ORANGE**

plaid

YELLOW

stripes

mix: **YELLOW + BLUE GREEN**

BLUE

checks

waterfall

cave

fish

boulder

What color is: **RED + BLUE** ?

BROWN

Does red make
a bull angry?

Ask your parents
why the sky is blue.
Boy, will they have trouble
with that one!

rainbow

canary

bluejay

cardinal

tulips

roses

black-eyed
Susans

daffodils

bumblebee

poppies

39

Big and Little

Big and little,
Short and tall,
Fat and thin,
And that's not all.
Crooked and straight,
Round and square,
You can see something -
But nothing's not there.

41

For Your Head

king's crown

toupee

moustache

queen's crown

hair ribbon

eyeglasses

sunglasses

beard

wig

football helmet

pith helmet

chef's hat

ponytail

army helmet

earphones

sailor hat

baseball cap

catcher's mask

makeup

fire fighter's helmet

hummingbird

earrings

top hat

bonnet

42

rubbers

baseball glove

knee socks

sneakers

flippers

roller skates

hiking boots

boxing gloves

high-heeled shoes

cowboy boots

mittens

ring

high-top sneakers

wooden shoes

nail polish

sandals

argyle socks

For Your Hands and Feet

fuzzy slippers

gloves

snowshoes

rubber boots

surfboard

stilts

pogo stick

slip

dress

undershirt

under pants

belt

necktie

bow tie

suit

vest

suspenders

trousers

turtleneck

blouse

necklace

bracelet

skirt

swimming suit

swimming trunks

shirt

tank top

hula hoop

T-shirt

For Your Middle

shorts

bathrobe

44

Dress-Up

helmet

sword

eye patch

water pistol

cowboy hat

COWBOY

banner

deerstalker hat

cowboy boots

KNIGHT

shield

magnifying glass

ten-gallon hat

PIRATE

headdress

bow and arrow

trench coat

bandana

DETECTIVE

INDIAN

hobby horse

BANDIT

scooter

MONSTER

crown

MAD SCIENTIST

test tubes

microscope

flask

royal robe

laboratory coat

DADDY

MOMMY

KING AND QUEEN

KING

QUEEN

cape

Boy is that a funny mask.

SUPERHERO

That's no mask. It's my face.

45

Numbers

1 little thing

2 trollusks running

3 sleeping kerploppuses

4 peeping eyeballs

5 devils laughing

6 useless blobs

7 broken windows

8 squirmy snakes

9 beasts bellowing

10 little specks

11 creatures creeping

12 trolls' warts

13 eggs hatching

14 toads

15 scowling skulls

16 witches' hats

17 forked tails

18 bat wings

19 muddy footprints

20 pointed fangs

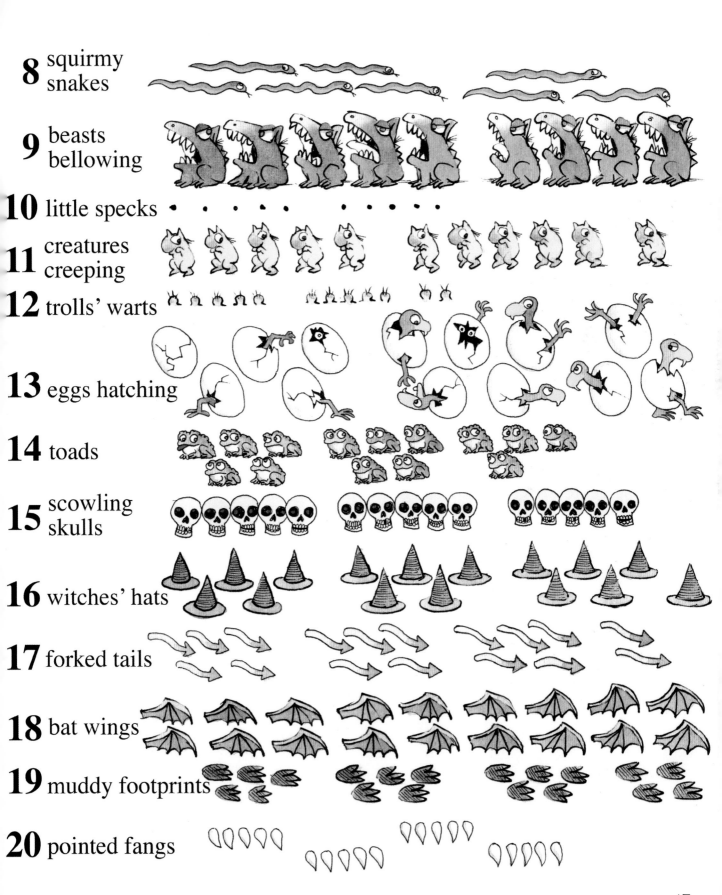

47

Mercer Mayer's
Little Monster®

Mother Goose

ACT ONE·

Donkey, donkey old and gray,
Open your mouth and gently bray;
Lift your ears and blow your horn,
To wake the world this sleepy morn.

If I had a donkey that wouldn't go,
Would I beat him? Oh, no, no.
I'd put him in the barn and give him some corn,
The best little donkey that ever was born .

Dingty, diddlety,
My mammy's maid;
She stole oranges,
I'm afraid.
Some in her pocket,
Some in her sleeve;
She stole oranges,
I do believe.

57

The cock's in the woodpile
Blowing his horn;
The bull's in the barn
A-threshing the corn.
The maid's in the meadow
A-making the hay;
The Croonies in the river
Are swimming away.

Margaret wrote a letter,
Sealed it with her finger,
Threw it in the dam
For the dusty miller.
Dusty was his coat,
Dusty was the silver,
Dusty was the kiss
I'd from the dusty miller.
If I had my pockets
Full of gold and silver,
I would give it all
To my dusty miller.

Little girl, little girl,
Where have you been?
I've been to see Grandmother
Over the green.
What did she give you?
Milk in a can.
What did you say for it?
"Thank you, Grandam."

Hie to the market, Jenny come trot,
Spilt all her buttermilk, every drop.
Every drop and every dram,
Jenny came home with an empty can.

61

Hearts, like doors, will open with ease
To very, very little keys;
And don't forget that two of these
Are "I thank you" and "If you please."

When I was a little boy
I had but little wit;
'Tis a long time ago,
And I have no more yet;
Nor ever, ever shall,
Until I die,
For the longer I live
The more fool am I.

Leg over leg,
As the Kerploppus went to Dover,
When he came to a pail,
Jump he went over.

Rain on the green grass,
And rain on the tree,
Rain on the house-top.
But not on me.

Evening red and morning gray,
Send the traveller on his way;
Evening gray and morning red,
Bring the rain upon his head.

Old King Cole was a merry old soul,
And a merry old soul was he;
He called for his pipe, and he called for his bowl,
And he called for his fiddlers three.

Every fiddler, he had a fine fiddle,
And a very fine fiddle had he;
Twee, tweedle-dee, tweedle-dee, went the fiddlers.
Oh, there's none so rare as can compare
With King Cole and his fiddlers three.

Cobbler, cobbler, mend my shoe,
Get it done by half past two;
Stitch it up and stitch it down,
Then I'll give you half a crown.

Matthew, Mark, Luke, and John,
Hold this donkey till I leap on.
Hold him steady, hold him sure,
And I'll get over the misty moor.

Little Monster, fellow fine,
Can you shoe this horse of mine?
Yes, good sir, that I can,
As well as any other man.
There's a nail and there's a prod,
And now, good sir. your horse is shod.

If I'd as much money as I could spend,
I never would cry, "Old chairs to mend!
Old chairs to mend! Old chairs to mend!"
I never would cry, "Old chairs to mend!"

If I'd as much money as I could tell,
I never would cry, "Old clothes to sell!
Old clothes to sell! Old clothes to sell!"
I never would cry, "Old clothes to sell!"

Little Miss Muffet
Sat on a tuffet,
Eating her curds and whey;
There came a great spider,
Who sat down beside her,
And frightened Miss Muffet away.

There was a little boy went into a barn,
And lay down on some hay;
An owl came out and flew about,
And the little boy ran away.

75

Hark! Hark! The dogs do bark,
Beggars are coming to town;
Some in rags and some in tags,
And some in velvet gowns.

Christmas is coming,
The geese are getting fat;
Please to put a penny
In the old dragon's hat.
If you haven't got a penny.
A ha'penny will do;
If you haven't got a ha'penny,
Then God bless you!

Moll-in-the-Wad and I yell out,
And what do you think it was all about?
I gave her a shilling, she swore it was bad,
"It's an old soldier's button," said Moll-in-the-Wad.

Naughty paughty Jack-a-Dandy
Stole a piece of sugar candy
From the grocer's shoppy-shop,
And away did hoppy-hop.

There was an old woman lived under the hill,
And if she's not gone she lives there still.
Baked apples she sold, and cranberry pies,
And she's the old woman that never told lies.

One thing at a time
And that done well,
Is a very good rule,
As many can tell.

This little monster
Went to market,
This little monster
Stayed home,

This little monster
Had roast beef,
This little monster
Had none,

And this little monster cried,
"Wee, wee, wee!"
All the way home.

Wee, wee, wee.

That's it, I'm leaving!

Hickory, dickory, dock,
There's a Croonie on the clock.
The clock struck three,
The Croonie did flee,
Hickory, dickory, dee.

83

Sing a song of sixpence,
A pocket full of rye;
Four-and-twenty black bats
Baked in a pie.

84

When the pie was opened,
The bats began to sing;
Wasn't that a messy dish
To set before the King?

The King was in the countinghouse,
Counting out his money;
The Queen was in the parlor,
Eating bread and honey;
The maid was in the garden,
Hanging out the clothes;
When down came a Bombanat
And snipped off her nose.

Rub-a-dub-dub,
Three men in a tub;
And who do you think they be?
The butcher, the baker,
The candlestick-maker;
Turn 'em out, knaves all three!

This little pig had a rub-a-dub,
This little pig had a scrub-a-scrub,
This little pig-a-wig ran upstairs,
This little pig-a-wig called out, "Bears!"
Down came the jar with a loud slam! Slam!
And this little pig had all the jam.

Wee Willie Winkie runs through the town,
Upstairs and downstairs, in his nightgown;
Rapping at the window, crying through the lock,
"Are the children all in bed, for now it's eight o'clock."

I see the moon,
And the moon sees me;
God bless the moon,
And God bless me.

Letters

Angry
anchovy

Big bite

Cup of cola

Down the drain

Eat everything

Fetch the fiddle

Give a grin

Hold him

It is icky

Jumping
jack-in-the-box

Kicking
kerploppus

Leaping
lizards

Much
mud